I SU

THE GREAT ALASKA EARTHQUAKE, 196

I SURVIVED

I SURVIVED

THE GREAT ALASKA EARTHQUAKE, 1964

by Lauren Tarshis

illustrated by Scott Dawson

Scholastic Inc.

Photos ©: 99: Jeff Schultz/Newscom; 100: Wulff (Barry) Collection, Valdez Museum & Historical Archive; 103: Courtesy of Tom Gilson; 105: Courtesy of Dorothy Moore; 112: NOAA Central Photo Library; 113 top: Science History Images/Alamy Stock Photo; 113 bottom: U.S. Geological Survey; 115: NOAA Central Photo Library; 117: NICHOLAS KAMM/AFP via Getty Images; 119: GraphicsRF.com/Shutterstock; 121: U.S. Geological Survey; 121, 126 icons: Vectorstock1/Shutterstock; 123: Ned Rozell; 124: ZUMA Press Inc/Alamy Stock Photo; 126: Jim McMahon/Mapman ®; 129: Dzmltry/Shutterstock; 130: Tomas Nevesely/Shutterstock; 132: THONY BELIZAIRE/AFP/Getty Images. All other photos by David Dreyfuss.

Special thanks to Henry Fountain, Tom Gilson, Dorothy Moore, Caron Oberg, Faith Revell, and Caroline Wiseman.

This book is being published simultaneously in hardcover by Scholastic Press.

ISBN 978-1-338-89178-2

10 9 8 7 6 5 4 3 2 1

23 24 25 26 27

Printed in the U.S.A.   40
First printing 2023
Designed by Katie Fitch

For Pops

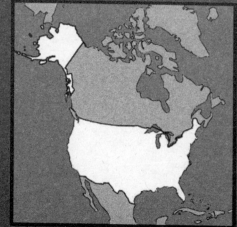

ARCTIC OCEAN

RUSSIA

ALASKA

CANADA

BERING SEA

VALDEZ
ANCHORAGE
GLENNALLEN
Copper River

Prince William
Sound

JUNEAU

PACIFIC OCEAN

N
W   E
S

CHAPTER 1

FRIDAY, MARCH 27, 1964
5:36 P.M.
VALDEZ, ALASKA

To eleven-year-old Jackson Barrett, it seemed like the world was ending.

He was caught in the middle of the most powerful earthquake in United States history. Across Alaska, the ground shattered like glass. Buildings fell to pieces. Icy cliffsides crashed into the sea. Giant tsunami waves smashed into towns and villages along the coast.

Just moments before it started, Jackson had been at the waterfront in the small town of Valdez. The docks were crowded with families and happy kids. Suddenly, a strange roar filled the air. Jackson's body shook. But wait . . . it wasn't just his body that was shaking. Everything around him was shaking, too.

And then a woman screamed.

"Earthquake!"

The roaring got louder, hammering Jackson's ears. The ground shook harder, knocking him down to his knees. The freezing water in the harbor seemed to boil like an evil witch's brew. On the streets, cars swerved and spun. Trees and telephone poles swayed.

The roaring got louder. The shaking got harder.

Louder. Harder. Louder. Harder.

Jackson tried to stand up, but it was impossible. The ground seemed to have come alive — rising and falling, twisting and rolling. For Jackson, it was like riding on top of a giant squirming snake.

He clawed his way forward on his hands and knees, inching his way across the shaking ground. He had finally made it out to the street when . . .

Crack!

A massive gash opened in the ground right in front of him.

Jackson turned around, but . . .

Crack!

An even bigger gash tore open behind him.

A sickening stench rose from the darkness below. Jackson tried not to think of what could be waiting for him down there.

Boiling lava? Shooting flames? The slobbering mouth of a hungry beast?

The ground under him started to crumble apart.

"Please, please, nooooooooooooooooooo!" Jackson screamed.

But down he fell, helpless and terrified, into the darkness.

CHAPTER 2

THREE WEEKS EARLIER
MONDAY, MARCH 9, 1964
4:30 IN THE AFTERNOON
120 MILES FROM VALDEZ,
DEEP IN THE WILDERNESS

"I don't think we'll be having fish for dinner tonight," Mom said, flicking a small icicle from her eyelash.

Jackson peered down into the hole he and Dad had chopped through the thick river ice. They'd been fishing for hours. So far, not even a nibble.

Needles of cold jabbed at Jackson's toes. It wasn't too cold today — around 5 degrees. But he still should have worn a third pair of socks.

Jackson stared down into the dark water. "I know you're down there, fish!"

Dad chuckled, and Mom let out one of her famous barking laughs. She sounded like a seal. "A very jolly seal," Dad always said.

It was that laugh that had caught Dad's attention all those years ago, when he and Mom were in college in Ohio. Back then, Dad was already dreaming of living on his own in the Alaskan bush. That's what people called the wild parts of Alaska that were far from roads and towns. It turned out Mom was ready for an adventure, too. They came up here after college, found a patch of land near the river, and started building the cabin.

What a disaster!

Eying his parents, Jackson thought of all the horror stories they'd told him about their first year in the bush. They ran out of food halfway through the winter. They got lost in the forest and nearly froze. Mom ate a poisonous mushroom and puked her guts out for a week. Finally, it was summer — and they were practically eaten alive by swarms of bloodthirsty Alaska mosquitoes.

"We were idiots," Mom liked to say. "We had no idea what we were doing."

"We almost died ten times," Dad would add, shaking his head.

But each mistake taught Mom and Dad something new. And when they weren't hungry or freezing or being devoured by bloodsuckers, they were falling more and more in love with each other — and with the wild land around them. Jackson was born two years later. He'd spent his whole life in the tiny cabin Mom and Dad had built about two miles from the river.

Lucky me, Jackson thought, smiling to himself and giving his freezing toes a wriggle.

"So, what should we have for dinner?" Dad asked.

"How about moose stew," Mom said. "Or we could have moose burgers or moose meatloaf . . . or moose meatballs."

"Or moose chili?" Jackson asked.

"Oh, that would hit the spot," Dad said.

"Moose chili it is," Mom said.

By this time of year, they were all sick to death of moose meat. It was their main food in the winter. Most other animals they could eat were hiding underground or hibernating during the coldest months. One male moose had six hundred pounds of meat. They'd hunt one down, butcher the animal, cut up the meat, and preserve it in jars they sealed shut in boiling water.

By now Jackson had eaten so much moose meat he was surprised he didn't have antlers. But he never complained. Three years ago, they couldn't find a moose before winter blasted in. They barely had any meat all winter. Luckily, they had their winter supply of rice and beans and noodles.

But they had to be careful. Because if they ran out, they couldn't just drive to a store. They had no car. There were no roads in the bush. The nearest store was in a town about twenty miles away.

No, living here wasn't always easy. Their cabin had no electricity or running water; their toilet was a hole in the ground. The forest was filled with grizzlies and wolves.

A person had to be tough to live in the bush — Alaska tough.

Jackson looked around now, shivering a little. His toes were numb. But he smiled to himself as he looked up the river. It curled like an icy blue ribbon through the thick green forest. He'd always felt lucky to live in such an amazing place.

. . .

Mom led the way on the two-mile journey back home. The sun was starting to go down when the cabin finally came into sight. It was small and plain — just four walls made of logs, with moss stuffed into the cracks to keep out the cold.

They were a few steps from the front porch when Mom stopped short.

"What's wrong?" Dad asked.

Mom pointed at something in the snow: huge paw prints, scattered all around them.

Jackson's stomach clenched as Dad slid his rifle off his shoulder.

Only one animal left a track like that.

A grizzly.

CHAPTER 3

Jackson dropped to his knees and studied one of the paw prints. It was massive — bigger than his own two hands put together. The toes were spread about an inch apart. Above each toe print was a dot. Those were where the tips of the bear's slashing claws dug deep into the snow.

Grizzly for sure. Jackson had learned to read animal tracks before he'd learned his ABCs.

"This makes no sense," Jackson said, standing up. "How could a grizzly be here?"

At this time in March, bears were supposed to still be hibernating.

During the fall, they gorged themselves on roots and fish and whatever food they could find. Then they curled up in hollow trees or beneath rocky ledges and went into a kind of sleep. They stayed hidden away until at least late April.

That was one good thing about winter in Alaska — not worrying about grizzlies.

"It's a winter bear," Mom said in a low voice.

The two words — *winter bear* — turned Jackson's blood to ice.

It was what they called a grizzly that came out of hibernation before it was supposed to. Winter bears were rare — Jackson had never seen one with his own eyes. But he'd heard terrifying stories about bears that crawled out of their dens way too early, desperately hungry.

But where could a bear find food in the winter? Fish were sealed away under the thick ice. Small animals were tunneled into winter dens, deep below the frozen ground. Berry bushes were bare. That's why winter bears found their way to cabins, to humans. It was rare for a grizzly bear to attack a person. But winter bears were different. They would eat anything — or anyone — they could find.

"Stay close together," Mom said now. Dad clutched his rifle. He'd never shoot an animal unless he had a good reason. Jackson hoped this wasn't one of those times.

Jackson narrowed his eyes, searching for the bear in the gathering darkness. He saw a pile of its scat — grizzly poop — and more huge paw prints. But he couldn't see the bear anywhere.

"Could it be gone?" Mom asked.

Jackson's hopes rose.

But then came a loud crash from inside the cabin.

Jackson's heart stopped. The winter bear . . . that beast was in their home!

"We have to stop it!" Mom cried, lunging forward.

"Deb!" Dad barked, grabbing Mom's arm. "You know that's too dangerous!"

"But, Bruce, all our food . . ."

The jars that filled their kitchen shelves — the

preserved moose meat, jams, and berries. The can of salmon they were saving for Dad's birthday next month. Bags and boxes of rice and beans and noodles. The grizzly would knock all the jars onto the floor, shattering the glass. It would slash through the bags and boxes, bite through the cans. The bear would eat all it could. What it left behind would be filthy and ruined.

Jackson took a breath, trying to calm himself. But then he heard other sounds.

Crackle. Pop.

Jackson's eyes widened as smoke started seeping from under the front door of the cabin.

"Fire!" Jackson shouted.

Dad whispered a curse. "The bear must have knocked over the stove!"

Their heavy metal stove, which kept them warm, where Mom cooked their food. They always tamped down the fire before they left the cabin. But a grizzly could have knocked it over, scattering glowing embers, bits of wood that could ignite a fire.

Whoosh!

Jackson leapt back as flames shot through the cabin roof. The darkening sky glowed bloodred, and showers of sparks filled the air. Panic shot through Jackson's body. But there was nothing he — or anyone — could do. There was no fire department here. No neighbors to rush over with buckets and hoses.

Suddenly, the cabin door burst open. The grizzly staggered through a curtain of smoke.

The bear was small and thin. One of its pointed ears was ragged and torn. It looked at them and let out a weak, rasping cry.

Dad aimed his rifle, but the bear vanished into the darkness.

Jackson stared ahead as the cabin crumbled away inside the orange, twisting flames. Everything he and Mom and Dad owned was inside — not just the food, but clothes, Jackson's homeschooling books and supplies, quilts Mom had sewn, furniture Jackson had helped Dad build.

Soon it would all be gone.

And what about Mom and Dad and Jackson? What would happen to them?

How would they even make it through this freezing night?

CHAPTER 4

Jackson fought tears and tried to steady his heart. It was beating so hard he could hear it pounding in his ears.

Boom! Boom! Boom!

Mom must have heard it, too.

"Hey," she said, gripping his shoulders. "We're going to be all right."

Jackson wanted to believe Mom. But how would they be all right? Without their cabin they'd freeze. Without their food they'd starve. And what if the winter bear came back? Jackson stared at the burning cabin, as if the answer might appear through the flames and smoke.

"You know what we have to do," Mom said in a low voice. "We have to get to work."

Get to work.

That was a Barrett family saying, almost like a prayer. It was what they said when something bad happened, when all you wanted to do was curl into a ball and give up.

It meant, Get a grip on yourself. Stop whining. Get busy staying alive.

Like that day last winter when Jackson was out rabbit hunting on his own. He'd been about a mile from the cabin when suddenly the sky got dark. Gray clouds cracked open. Snow poured down in thick sheets. Jackson couldn't see two inches ahead of him. There was no way he'd make it home.

Jackson was so scared he couldn't think straight. He'd run through the trees, slipped, and then *bam!* Down he went, hard, onto his back. He'd struggled to his feet, then stomped around blindly until he tripped again. *Bam!* This time he fell flat on his face. He bit his tongue so hard his mouth filled with blood.

He lay there as the snow poured down. *I'm done*, he'd thought.

Dad once told Jackson that there were a thousand ways to die in Alaska. He'd meant it as a kind of joke. There definitely weren't one thousand. Probably more like fifty. And freezing to death in a blizzard had to be in the top five. Blinded by snow, people roamed around and around in circles until they were too exhausted to take another step. Finally, they dropped to the ground and gave up. Their bodies disappeared under a blanket of snow until the spring, when the wolves and vultures found them . . . and picked their bones clean.

Jackson had imagined his own shining bones. *That's going to be me!* he'd thought.

And then a voice had whispered through his mind.

Get to work!

And then louder . . .

Get to work!

His mind suddenly cleared. He'd stood up and slipped off his beat-up army backpack, which was packed with emergency supplies.

A compass and flashlight in case he got lost. Emergency matches for building a fire. Moose jerky and dried blueberries for energy. A whistle to scare away threatening animals. A rope to lower himself down from cliffs. And a shovel . . . in case he ever got caught in a blizzard.

Jackson had used the shovel to dig himself a big hole under a spruce tree. When the hole was good and deep, he'd climbed inside. He'd tugged his parka hood over his head and pulled his knees to his chest. Huddled in his little snow cave, he'd stayed surprisingly warm and dry.

After two hours, the snow stopped.

Jackson would never forget the looks on Mom's and Dad's faces when he walked through the cabin door, how quickly their worry turned to pride. That was the moment Jackson knew he was tough. Alaska tough.

And right now, as the hissing fire destroyed their cabin, Jackson dug deep for that feeling again.

Yes, it was freezing cold. Overnight it would

get even colder. The winter bear was still out there. That's why he couldn't waste time standing around whimpering.

Jackson took a big breath and stood taller.

"Okay," he said to Mom. "Let's get to work."

CHAPTER 5

About twenty yards from the cabin were two big steel drums, each the size of a large garbage can. Dad used his knife to pry open the bear-proof lids. Inside was everything they needed to keep from freezing and starving to death: a sturdy tent, sleeping bags, flashlights, a first aid kit, a camping stove, and a pot to melt snow for water. Plus, there was enough moose jerky to feed them for a few days.

Of course Mom and Dad had made sure they were prepared — even for this.

The sounds of the fire filled the air.

Sizzle. Crackle. Hiss.

Boom! A window shattered. The thick smoke burned Jackson's nose. Falling embers sizzled as they brushed against his face.

But Jackson ignored the sounds and the smells and the pinpricks of pain. He barely glanced at the fire's twisting flames. He kept his mind focused on the work of loading the supplies onto the sled. When everything was piled on top, they dragged it to a spot far from the cabin. That way they'd be safe from flying sparks and embers.

As they set up the tent, Mom and Dad worked out their plan.

"We'll stay here tonight," Dad said, grabbing a tent pole. "At sunrise we'll leave for Glennallen."

That was the closest town, twenty miles away. In the summer, they'd take their canoe down the river and get there in a day. But it was winter, and the river was frozen. They'd have to walk — a three-day journey.

If they were lucky.

Jackson tried not to imagine what could happen to them on such a long trek in the winter. They could get slammed by a blizzard. They could fall through river ice. And that winter bear . . .

But he understood why they couldn't just stay here and live in their tent. It was too cold. And just like that winter bear, they wouldn't be able to find enough food. The calendar said that the first day of spring was only a couple of weeks away. What a joke. Here in Alaska, the freezing weather could stick around for months after that.

"We'll call Uncle Solly from the general store," Mom said, spreading out a tarp over the snowy ground. "He'll drive up to Glennallen to get us."

Uncle Solly. Just hearing that name helped Jackson relax. Uncle Solly was Mom and Dad's best friend — Jackson's, too. He lived in Valdez, a busy town on the sea about one hundred miles south of Glennallen.

Jackson, Mom, and Dad stayed in Valdez with Uncle Solly every summer. Those three-week trips were a chance to take a short break from the wilderness. They'd stock up on food for the winter, see the doctor and the dentist, and go on adventures with Uncle Solly.

Uncle Solly lived in a small cottage not far from the busy Valdez waterfront. Jackson felt like a prince as he took hot showers and used the toilet — which was inside the house! And the store-bought food! Milk. Eggs. Chips. Cookies. Ice cream. Jackson stuffed himself at every meal.

But three weeks in Valdez was always enough for Jackson. The noise, the cars, the people . . . it was all too much. He never liked saying goodbye to Uncle Solly. But he couldn't wait to get back home to the quiet of the bush.

"How long will we stay in Valdez?" Jackson asked as he pounded a tent pole into the frozen ground.

"Dad and I will have to get jobs," Mom said. "We're going to need to save up money to buy supplies to rebuild."

"Maybe we can get back here by August," Dad said.

Four months.

Already that seemed like forever.

CHAPTER 6

FOUR DAYS LATER
FRIDAY, MARCH 13, 1964
4:45 A.M.
VALDEZ, ALASKA

Rooooooooooaaaaar!

The winter bear was in the cabin! And now it had come for Jackson, and there was no escape. Jackson stared in horror at the bear's dripping teeth, smelled its bloody breath. He braced himself for the bone-crunching bite.

And then . . . Jackson's eyes snapped open.

It took a few seconds for his groggy head to clear.

There was no bear. He wasn't in the cabin. He and Mom and Dad had made it to Valdez last night. They'd gone to sleep in Uncle Solly's attic guest room.

Jackson could hear Mom and Dad breathing softly from their bed a few feet away. In the moonlight, he could see the clock on the dresser — 4:45 A.M.

Jackson pulled the quilt around him. He shivered as he remembered the three bitterly cold nights they'd spent in their tent. His bones and muscles ached from the twenty-mile walk. But they'd been lucky. No blizzards. No sign of the winter bear.

They'd made it to Glennallen with no trouble. The owners of the general store made them bowls of chili while they waited for Uncle Solly.

By sunset last night, they were finally here, safe and sound.

Jackson eyed the clock again. Should he get out of bed now? Back home Jackson was always up at five o'clock. That way he could do some of his homeschool work before chores. But his school supplies and books were all burned up now. It felt so good to be warm. *Just a few more minutes*, Jackson thought, closing his eyes.

The next time Jackson woke up, the sun was streaming through the window. Mom and Dad's bed was empty. He looked at the clock. What?! Eight o'clock?! He'd never slept that late in his life! One night in Valdez and already he'd turned into a lazy slug.

He scrambled out of bed and threw on his clothes. They stank of smoke and sweat and moose jerky. In a flash he was down the stairs.

"Good morning!" Uncle Solly boomed when Jackson walked into the cozy kitchen. He was at the stove. Mom and Dad were sipping coffee at the table. Jackson was glad to see his parents looking cheerful and bright eyed. They'd all been dragging last night when they finally got to Valdez.

"Sorry I slept so late," Jackson said.

"I could have slept all day," Mom said with a yawn.

"Be glad you weren't up early," Uncle Solly said to Jackson. "You escaped helping me shovel the driveway. It snowed last night. Again."

Jackson looked out the window.

Whoa! There was at least a foot of fresh snow, on top of the five feet that had been there last night. Drifts rose up past the first-floor window of the house next door.

"Did you know we get more snow here in Valdez than anywhere else in Alaska?" Uncle Solly said as he cracked an egg into a sizzling skillet.

Dad and Mom smirked at Jackson over their mugs of coffee. Uncle Solly loved reminding them that Valdez was extra special.

"Most beautiful town in Alaska," he would brag. "Everyone agrees."

Out the window, Jackson could see straight down the street to the waterfront. Fishing boats bobbed in the bright blue water. Across the harbor, a zigzag of sparkling mountains rose into the morning sky. It was pretty, Jackson thought. But he missed the pine trees that surrounded the cabin.

Uncle Solly put a heaping plate of fluffy eggs,

thick bacon, and toast in front of Jackson. *Now, that is beautiful*, Jackson thought. They never got to eat eggs at the cabin. And Uncle Solly's toast was made with the squishy white store-bought bread Jackson loved.

"Thanks, Uncle Solly," Jackson said as he shoveled the first forkful into his mouth.

"You won't believe it," Mom said, sitting back in her chair. "Dad and I already have jobs!"

"How did that happen?" Jackson asked through a mouthful.

"Uncle Solly hired us," Dad said.

Uncle Solly turned from the stove, his smile bright under his big bushy mustache. He was a carpenter, and it turned out he needed help with a new house he was building.

"I'm lucky you showed up," he said.

"We're the lucky ones," Mom said, smiling at Uncle Solly. "You've always been there for us."

That was true. Mom and Dad had met Uncle Solly during their miserable first year in Alaska. He was living in the bush back then, in a cabin about six miles from theirs. When Mom and Dad ran out of food that winter, Uncle Solly shared his. He'd taught them about hunting and fishing and living off the land. Without Uncle Solly's help, Mom and Dad always said, they wouldn't have survived the winter.

"Uncle Solly," Jackson said, swallowing his last bite of eggs. "I'll help with that house, too."

It was the least he could do to show his thanks to Uncle Solly. Plus, he needed more practice if he was going to help Mom and Dad rebuild the cabin.

"Jackson," Mom said. "You're not going to have time to work. You'll be in school."

"I can get my schoolwork done early in the morning," Jackson said, mopping up the last of his eggs with a crust of toast. He and Mom had always managed to squeeze three or four hours of school into their busy days.

"We can't homeschool from here," Mom said. "I'm going to be working too much. Dad and I are going to sign you up at the elementary school down the street. You'll start Monday."

Jackson dropped his toast.

"I can't do that!" he said.

He'd never set foot inside an actual school. But he knew what it would be like: A grumpy grandma type as a teacher. Lessons so boring he'd fall asleep. Six hours a day stuck at a desk. Jackson was used to spending his days outside, always on the move.

Going to school would be like being in jail!

"Come on," Dad said with a frown. "Millions of kids go to school every day."

"It's only for a couple of months," Mom said. "You'll make some friends."

Jackson didn't need friends, thank you. He'd always gotten by on his own. And besides, what did he have in common with stuck-up town kids?

He opened his mouth to explain all this. But then he shut it again. Mom and Dad had made up their minds.

And Jackson wasn't a whiner. He'd made it through a blizzard. He'd trudged twenty miles in the freezing cold.

He was pretty sure he was tough enough for fifth grade.

CHAPTER 7

"Welcome, Jackson! I'm Miss Lawrence. Please come in!"

Jackson stood in the doorway of the classroom and tried to hide his surprise. This teacher was no grumpy grandma type. She was young and tall, with long black hair and a bright smile.

Jackson scanned the classroom. It was sunny,

with colorful maps and posters on the walls. About twenty kids sat at desks lined up in rows.

The boys all had short hair and were dressed in neat shirts and pants. Jackson glanced at his rumpled secondhand flannel shirt Mom had found yesterday in a church used-clothes bin. He patted down his overgrown curls — maybe he should have cut his hair.

Too late now.

"Class, this is Jackson," Miss Lawrence said brightly.

"Hello, Jackson," the class all said together.

Jackson's stomach started to churn, and the pancakes and two glasses of milk from breakfast sloshed around in his stomach.

Was he going to puke? All over the floor? He'd never been to school before. But he was pretty sure puking was the worst thing that could happen to a kid.

He took a breath . . . *Get a grip*.

Miss Lawrence led him to the closet where he could hang his coat and leave his lunchbox. He took off his beat-up army backpack, still filled with his emergency supplies. No, he probably didn't need them here in Valdez. But you never knew.

Miss Lawrence pointed out an empty desk in the middle of the room. As Jackson sat down, a girl with short brown hair and cat-eye glasses leaned over and smiled.

"I'm Leonor."

"I'm Chris," said a short but muscular boy with fox-colored hair.

"I'm Nora," whispered a smiling girl with long yellow braids.

"I'm Mary," said the rosy-cheeked girl next to her.

Other kids looked at Jackson and waved.

None of them seemed stuck-up, as far as Jackson could tell.

"Jackson," Miss Lawrence said, "you're just in time for our morning geography lesson. Is everyone ready?"

"Yes, Miss Lawrence!" everyone sang.

She stood in front of a big map of Alaska that hung in the front of the room.

Jackson's stomach settled. Finally, the kids weren't all staring at him.

"Alaska's capital is . . . ?" Miss Lawrence said.

"Juneau!" chanted the class.

"Biggest city?"

"Anchorage!"

"When did Alaska become a state?"

"1959!"

"When did people first come to Alaska?"

It was quiet for a few seconds.

A few kids tried.

"In the 1800s, during the gold rush!"

Miss Lawrence shook her head.

"1700s, Russian explorers?"

"No . . ." Miss Lawrence said.

"During the Ice Age!" Nora called out.

Miss Lawrence smiled. "Yes."

Wow, Jackson thought. That was a long time ago.

"Nobody knows exactly when the first people came to Alaska," Miss Lawrence said. "But it was definitely more than ten thousand years ago. And some of those people were my ancestors. As you all know, I am Unangax̂."

That's one of the main Alaskan Native Cultural groups, Jackson thought, thinking back to the books he and Mom had read about Alaska. *There are many groups — Inupiaq, St. Lawrence Island Yupik, Yup'ik, Cup'ik, Athabascan, Eyak, Tsimshian, Tlingit, Haida, Sugpiaq . . . and each is different. They have different languages and customs, different myths and arts.*

"Hey, Miss Lawrence!" Chris said with a sneaky grin. "You don't look ten thousand years old!"

Kids giggled, and Miss Lawrence let out a big laugh — almost as loud as Mom's.

"I was not born during the Ice Age, thank you," she said.

"Where did your ancestors come from, Miss Lawrence?" Leonor asked.

Miss Lawrence pointed to a big piece of land across the sea from Alaska. "They came from here," she said. "Today it's called Siberia."

She went on to explain that the sea between Siberia and Alaska was called the Bering Sea. "But back during the Ice Age, the land and oceans around the world looked very different. Part of the Bering Sea was dry land. So people could walk across to Alaska."

Staring at the map, Jackson tried to imagine what a hard journey that must have been. And what was Alaska like during the Ice Age? Even colder and icier than today. There were fewer trees to cut down and burn to stay warm. And even scarier animals. Like saber-toothed tigers, giant wolves, and bears twice as big as today's grizzlies. Jackson shuddered.

"Jackson," Miss Lawrence said, jolting Jackson out of his thoughts. "Where were you living before you came to Valdez?"

"Uh . . ." How should he answer that?

"About twenty miles from Glennallen," he said.

"Come up and show us on the map," Miss Lawrence said with a wave.

Jackson stood up. With every step toward the map, his beat-up work boots squeaked on the tiles.

He pushed his curls out of his eyes so he could

find Glennallen on the map. Then he pointed to a spot nearby where the blue line of the Copper River curved north.

Miss Lawrence stared. "How exciting! You were living in the bush!"

Jackson nodded.

"Wow!" someone shouted. Jackson thought it might be Chris.

"For how long?" Miss Lawrence asked.

"My whole life," Jackson said. "But our cabin

burned down a week ago. So that's why we're here . . ."

The ferocious winter bear from his nightmare flashed into Jackson's mind. His stomach twisted. This time he really was going to puke . . . for sure!

"Uh, be right back," Jackson muttered.

Then he bolted for the classroom door.

CHAPTER 8

Jackson ran down the halls. He'd seen the boys' room on his walk to the classroom. But now he couldn't find it. After three wrong turns he finally made it. He pushed his way into a stall and stood there. His heart pounded. Sweat dripped down his back. But the queasy feeling passed.

A minute later the outside door creaked open.

"Jackson?"

Miss Lawrence.

Jackson stepped out of the stall.

Miss Lawrence was right outside the boys' room, with the door open just a crack.

"Do you need to see the nurse?" she said.

Nurse?

Last winter Jackson nearly cut his finger off chopping wood. The blood soaked his shirt. Mom sewed up the deep cut with a needle and thread. Jackson bit down on a stick so he wouldn't yell out in pain with every stab of the needle.

Jackson didn't need a nurse for a queasy stomach.

"No, thank you," he said.

Miss Lawrence put her hand on his shoulder as they walked back to the classroom.

"You'll feel better," she said. "First days are hard . . ."

"Thanks," Jackson said, breaking away.

He knew Miss Lawrence was trying to be nice. But she didn't understand. He wasn't some spoiled town kid. He'd grown up in the bush.

The rest of the morning went okay. Luckily, kids didn't make a big deal about him rushing out of the room. Leonor leaned over and quietly asked him if he was okay, but that was it.

It turned out Jackson was way ahead of most

kids in math. He whipped through his long division problems. In grammar they worked on commas, which Mom had taught him about last year.

And the work wasn't boring. Miss Lawrence cracked jokes and even made stuff interesting. Jackson didn't fall asleep once. Plus, they had music class. Jackson didn't know any of the songs, but he liked listening to the other kids sing.

When it was time for lunch, the kids all took their lunchboxes to the cafeteria. The noise in there was louder than a thunderstorm in the bush. The giggles and shrieks of the kids. The shouts of the frazzled-looking teacher trying to get the little kids to stop throwing food. The banging of chairs and slamming of metal lunchboxes.

And Jackson had barely bitten into his bologna-and-cheese sandwich when kids started asking him questions about the bush.

"What did you eat?"

"Where did you sleep?"

"Did you have electricity?"

"How did you take a shower?"

Jackson answered as best he could. The kids were especially amazed to hear how he had to lug water from the creek just to wash dishes or take a bath.

"It sounds really fun!" Leonor said. "Like a camping trip."

Sure, Jackson thought. That's what Mom and Dad had thought when they first got to the bush. Then they almost died ten times. But no reason to tell these kids any of that.

"I don't know," Nora said, nibbling on a chip. "I couldn't live without electricity."

"I'd miss listening to music," Mary said.

In music class, Jackson had noticed that Mary had the best singing voice.

"I'd miss my Twinkies," Chris added, picking up one of the vanilla cakes and giving it a kiss.

The kids all laughed — even Jackson.

"What's the most amazing thing you've ever seen?" Leonor asked, leaning forward.

Jackson felt all their eyes on him, but surprisingly, he didn't get queasy like before.

He thought about some of his favorite

moments in the bush. A huge rainbow he saw after a big storm last summer. The sound of thousands of birds starting to sing at once right before a springtime sunrise. The time he saw an eagle snatch a huge salmon from the river with its pointy talon toes. To Jackson, every day in the bush was amazing.

But he was pretty sure these town kids didn't want to hear about sunsets and birds. They wanted blood, guts, and snarls.

Jackson had the perfect story.

CHAPTER 9

"I had spent the day fishing," Jackson said, wishing he could take all these kids back to that day. It was last June. The birds had come back from their winter getaways. Moose calves, fox kits, bear cubs, and baby rabbits were scampering around the forest with their mothers.

"On the way back to the cabin, I climbed up onto a high ridge that overlooked the valley."

That view popped into Jackson's mind — the endless green forest, the bright sparkle of the river, how the snow-topped mountains looked as if they were wearing diamond crowns.

"When I got to the top, I looked down. And right below me, maybe fifteen feet down, was a pack of wolves."

The kids all gasped.

"A whole pack!" Mary said.

"I'd pee my pants if I saw a wolf pack," Chris said.

Leonor elbowed him. "That's gross."

"Sorry!" Chris said. "It's true!"

Jackson understood why most people would be scared. Wolves were fierce predators — fast and tough, with jaws strong enough to bite through bones.

But Jackson shook his head.

"Wolves don't usually bother with humans," Jackson explained. At least not in the summer, when there was plenty of food. "Plus, I was up on those rocks — they couldn't get up there. And there was a strong wind blowing toward me. I could smell the wolves, but they couldn't pick up my scent."

Jackson could see the wolves so clearly. The

pups scampered around, tackling one another, rolling in the mud like furry little wrestlers. The grown-ups lounged in the sun like they didn't have a worry in the world.

"And then, out of nowhere, this huge grizzly came crashing out of the woods."

"Yikes!" Chris yelped. For a second, Jackson wondered if he should stop. Was this too scary for them?

"Go on!" Nora said, and the others nodded.

Guess not.

"The bear was massive," Jackson said. "I'd say it had to weigh a thousand pounds."

He remembered how the bear's muscles had rippled under its fur.

"Grizzlies are way bigger and stronger than wolves," Jackson pointed out. "One swipe of a grizzly's paw can crack a skull, or slice open a wolf's belly."

"That's gotta hurt!" Chris said with a wince.

"Poor wolves!" Mary cried.

"But here's the thing," Jackson said, lowering

his voice. It surprised him that the kids were so interested. "Wolves don't fight alone. They fight as a pack. They stick together."

He described how the grizzly went after one wolf, and how the other wolves came up behind the bear.

"They growled and snarled and snapped at the bear's legs. They stood their ground, protecting one another."

"Did it work?" Nora asked.

Jackson nodded. "The grizzly gave up eventually. It ran into the woods."

"The wolves win!" Chris cried out, raising his arms.

All the kids smiled.

"That was a really amazing story, Jackson," Leonor said.

"Better than a movie," Mary agreed.

Jackson sat back and took a deep breath. He was glad the kids liked his story. But he'd never talked so much in one day in his entire life. He could use some peace and quiet.

Except at recess the kids wanted to play hide-and-seek.

"Chris is it!" Nora shouted.

Jackson played for a while. But as the kids were scattered around hiding behind piles of snow, Jackson realized this was his chance to steal some time for himself.

He hurried all the way around the back of the school, far from the playground. He squeezed himself behind a shed and sat down. Finally, some peace.

"You're a good hider," Leonor said when the bell rang and Jackson finally came out of his spot.

The rest of the afternoon crept along. By three o'clock, Jackson's head was pounding. He couldn't wait to get home. But as he was putting on his parka, Chris came up to him.

"Jackson!" he said as he was zipping up. "Want to come with us to Leonor's?"

"She has the new Beatles," Nora said.

"The new . . . beetles?" Jackson asked, picturing shiny bugs inside a box. That made no sense.

Leonor must have noticed he was confused.

"They're a band!" She smiled. "The Beatles!"

How could he know that? And what a dumb name for a band!

"Wait until you hear their songs!" Mary said. "You'll love them!"

"And Leonor has a Hula-Hoop," Nora said.

Hula-Hoop? What in the world was that?

Back in the bush, Jackson could name any bird by listening to its song. He knew every flower by its smell. He could find his way home by looking at the sun or the stars.

But standing here, Jackson felt completely lost. His stomach started churning again.

"Come on," Nora said. "It will be fun. Leonor has some new Silly Putty."

Silly *what*?

He had to get out of here — now.

"Thanks," Jackson said, hurrying down the hallway. "But I need to get back home."

He rushed out of the classroom and down the hall. He pushed through the heavy front door of the school, sucking in the cold, fresh air.

Free!

He'd made it through his first day.

He tried not to think of how he would make it through the rest.

CHAPTER 10

TEN DAYS LATER
THURSDAY, MARCH 26, 1964

By the end of the second week, Jackson had
school figured out. He could remember all the
words to the Pledge of Allegiance. He'd learned
every verse of "My Country, 'Tis of Thee," which
they sang together after the pledge. He could get
to the boys' room with his eyes closed.

As for the kids, Jackson had decided it was
easier to just stay away. Half the time he didn't
understand what they were talking about. He'd

stand there feeling all confused, like a moose calf lost in the woods. What was the point of even trying to figure out what a Hula-Hoop was, or why this beetle band was so great? Soon he'd be back in the bush where he belonged. None of that stuff would matter. He'd never see these kids again.

At lunchtime he skipped the cafeteria and slipped right out to the playground. He'd pick out a quiet spot behind a giant pile of snow. That way he could eat his sandwich in peace.

He avoided the recess games of hide-and-seek. When Leonor would invite him over after school, Jackson would make up an excuse. Same with Mary's ice-skating party and sledding at Nora's.

Finally, kids stopped asking him to do things. They didn't try to include him in their talks about bands or toys or games. They didn't ask him to tell any more exciting stories about the bush. These past few days, nobody at school talked to Jackson much at all, except for Miss Lawrence.

Which was what Jackson wanted, right?

That Thursday morning, the class was buzzing with excitement. Easter weekend was coming up. School was closed tomorrow for the Good Friday holiday. All morning kids chattered about their holiday plans. There were family dinners. An Easter egg hunt. A basketball game at the high school. Ice-skating at the pond.

But what the kids were most excited about was a big supply ship that would be docking in Valdez tomorrow afternoon. It was called the *Chena*, and it was coming from Seattle. Jackson had already heard about it from Uncle Solly. His close buddy was a member of the crew. Uncle Solly was hoping to see him while the ship was docked.

"Half the town will be there to watch the *Chena* unload," Uncle Solly had said. "Everyone is waiting for something that's on that ship."

The stores in town were running low on food and other things, Uncle Solly had explained. Fresh fruits and vegetables. Toilet paper. Batteries. Parts for cars. Just yesterday Jackson had heard

Chris complaining that the market was out of Twinkies.

"I'm going to starve!" he'd moaned.

Pretty much everything people bought at stores in Alaska came from the Lower 48. That's what people in Alaska called the other parts of the United States — everywhere but Alaska and Hawaii.

Alaska had lots of trees and animals and fish, but not many farms or factories. Even Mom and Dad and Jackson needed to buy things. Like their parkas and boots, the kerosene for their lamps, their fishing gear and woodstove. And, of course, the extra food they needed for the winter — rice, noodles, oatmeal, beans. They wouldn't be able to live in the bush without all that stuff.

Thinking about all this, Jackson eyed Miss Lawrence as she wrote out long division problems on the blackboard. He tried to picture her ancestors trudging across that icy bridge. There were no stores or ships back then. People had to get everything from the land — every bite of food, every scrap of clothing. They invented new ways to hunt and fish. They figured out how to build warm houses and fast boats from caribou hide or the bark of trees. They'd found ways to live, to have families, to stay in Alaska for all these centuries.

Talk about Alaska tough, Jackson thought.

At recess that day, Jackson had found a new pile of snow where he could sit on his own. He'd just finished his sandwich when he heard kids talking nearby. He recognized some of the voices — Nora, Mary, Leonor, Chris. They couldn't see him, but he could hear what they were talking about.

"The *Chena* is the best ship," a boy was saying.

"Last year I got three lollipops," said Mary.

"I got chocolate!" said another girl.

"I got an orange," Nora said proudly.

An orange! Jackson had never even seen one of those.

He listened as Nora told how she brought it home and saved it for days.

"What did it taste like?" someone asked her.

"Like sunshine," she said.

Jackson smiled a little as he tried to imagine

what sunshine might taste like. Nora always knew how to describe things, Jackson had noticed.

The kids bickered over when it would be best to meet at the waterfront. In the end they decided on five o'clock.

"Should we invite Jackson?" Leonor asked.

Jackson's ears perked up. Maybe this was one time he'd say yes. He'd like to get his hands on a real orange.

"He won't come," Mary said.

"Don't even bother asking him," Nora said.

"Yeah," Chris added. "He hates us."

Jackson blinked, like he'd been slapped.

"That kid's weird," said another boy. "What's with that backpack? Who carries an army backpack to school?"

Jackson stared at his backpack.

"Don't be mean," Leonor said.

"Maybe he'd like us if we had fur and tails," Chris said.

A couple of kids snickered. Jackson's cheeks burned, like he was sitting too close to a fire.

The bell rang. Jackson heard the kids' crunching footsteps as they hurried back toward the school. He had to stop himself from chasing after them. *"I don't hate you!"* he wanted to shout.

But it was too late for that.

Because now they all hated him.

CHAPTER 11

THE NEXT DAY
FRIDAY, MARCH 27, 1964

Mom and Dad and Uncle Solly rushed through breakfast. Even though school was closed for Good Friday, they still had work to do on the house they were building. Jackson planned to spend the day doing chores for Uncle Solly. He hadn't slept well last night. Every time he'd closed his eyes, he'd heard the kids' voices from the playground.

"He hates us."

"That kid's weird."

"Maybe he'd like us if we had fur and tails."

Hopefully shoveling snow and splitting wood would help him clear his head.

"Jackson," Uncle Solly said as he was putting on his boots. "You remember that ship that's coming in this afternoon? The *Chena*?"

Jackson nodded. How could he forget?

"I need you to go down to the loading dock and get a note to my buddy in the crew. I'm not going to make it down to see him tonight. We're going to be working late at the house."

"Uh, sure," Jackson said.

Going down to the dock was the last thing Jackson wanted to do. Every kid in his class would be on that dock! But he couldn't say no to Uncle Solly. He'd just have to avoid the kids.

Uncle Solly scrawled out a note and handed it to Jackson.

"Just give it to any of the sailors you see," he said. "Get there around five thirty."

Would the kids be gone by then?

Jackson hoped so.

At five fifteen, Jackson grabbed his backpack and headed down to the waterfront. It was barely a five-minute walk. To distract himself, Jackson thought of all the fun times he'd had with Uncle Solly over the years. Heading out of the harbor in Uncle Solly's little boat, they'd explored the coves and bays tucked between the mountains.

There was always something to see — a walrus with dagger tusks, dolphins dancing in the waves, furry sea otters floating around on rafts they made from kelp.

Best of all was the humpback whale Jackson spotted a couple of years ago. It broke the surface of the bay — a massive creature more than fifty feet long. Water shot out of the blowhole on its back before it sank down again. A moment later, it exploded up out of the water. Arching its back, it seemed to hover in the air before disappearing in a shimmering splash that drenched Jackson and Uncle Solly.

Jackson's chest tightened as he thought of those happy summer days. He wondered what

Leonor would have said about that whale, or how Nora would have described it. Did Mary know any songs about whales? And what kind of joke would Chris have told to crack them all up?

Jackson would never know. And why should he care?

Jackson pulled his parka tighter around him as a bitter wind blew from the harbor. At least it wasn't snowing.

Jackson came to the end of Alaska Avenue. Just ahead of him was the waterfront. It was like a separate little town sitting right on the harbor — different docks, warehouses for fish and cargo, a salmon cannery where fish were cut up and packed into cans. Jackson could see the *Chena* floating with its right side up against the main loading dock. It was at least ten times as long as a humpback whale.

Jackson crossed a busy street and stepped onto a bridge that headed out over the water to the docks. Uncle Solly had been right; at least half the town was here. Cars were parked up and down the street. Kids skipped past Jackson, their parents chasing behind. A truck rumbled by and the bridge shook.

Jackson stepped off the bridge and onto the main loading dock. Dockworkers lugged crates into the warehouse. A forklift zipped past.

Jackson walked slowly toward the ship, reaching into his pocket for Uncle Solly's note. He looked around but didn't see any sailors to give it to. The only sailor he could see was above him, on the deck of the *Chena*. The man was

leaning over the railing, smiling down at a group of little kids gathered below.

"Who wants an apple?" he sang.

"I do!" cried a little girl in a pink hat. The man tossed the fruit down.

"Got it!" She clutched the apple to her chest like it was a gold nugget.

"How about a chocolate bar!" the man called.

"Me, me, me!" a little boy squealed.

Jackson watched until he spotted a sailor leaving the ship. Jackson hurried over to him and asked if he could deliver the note.

"Happy to!" the sailor said.

Jackson thanked him and darted away. Now he could get out of here!

But halfway across the bridge, Jackson spotted four kids walking toward him. Without a second look, he knew it was Leonor, Chris, Nora, and Mary. They were all laughing. Leonor gave Chris a playful push. Mary and Nora linked their arms together and skipped ahead.

Jackson remembered those scampering wolf

pups he'd watched from the cliff last summer. That's what these kids reminded him of. A wolf pack. He felt an ache in his chest — a lonely kind of ache. Wait . . . did he *want* to be part of their pack of kids?

No, he thought, pushing the idea away. It was better to be on his own.

But then why did he want to rush over to them?

Get a grip, Jackson thought. Those kids didn't want to see him. They hated him, right? Jackson slipped behind a parked car and squatted down behind it. He'd wait until they were out of sight and then hurry home, just like he'd planned.

As Jackson watched the kids walk by, those wolves popped back into his mind. He remembered their ferocious growls and snarls when the grizzly appeared. He could practically hear them.

Grrrrrrrrrrrrrrrrrrrr.

The sound got louder.

GRRRRRRRRRRRRRRRRRR.

But wait . . . that sound wasn't in his mind.

It was all around him.

What was happening? Jackson's body started to tremble. But no . . . it wasn't just his body shaking. *Everything* was shaking.

Suddenly, a woman screamed.

"Earthquake!"

CHAPTER 12

All at once, everyone who had been heading toward the docks rushed back toward the street. People screamed. Parents scooped up their children. Cars slammed on their brakes.

Jackson started to stand up to join the rush. His heart was beating a mile a minute. But then he squatted back down.

Earthquakes happen all the time, he reminded himself. There were more earthquakes here in Alaska than anywhere in the lower forty-eight states, even California.

In the bush, the ground would suddenly start

shaking. Trees would sway. Rabbits would dart out of their underground tunnels. Once, some jars of moose meat fell from their kitchen shelves and shattered on the floor.

But that was the worst earthquake damage Jackson had seen.

He braced himself against the parked car, expecting the earthquake to stop any moment.

It didn't.

The roaring got louder. The shaking got harder. Louder. Harder. Louder. Harder.

The water in the harbor began to churn and froth, like an evil witch's brew. Waves sloshed across the bridge. Fishing boats in the harbor bounced around like toys. The *Chena* strained against its thick ropes.

Louder. Harder. Louder. Harder.

The bridge was shaking so violently now that Jackson was bouncing up and down like a ball. His backpack slammed into his head over and over again. He braced himself against the car and glanced around for the other kids. Where had they gone? Hopefully off the bridge and back onto the street — which was where Jackson had to go.

He managed to stumble to the street. But then he fell again. And this time it was impossible to stand back up. The earth seemed to be alive — rising and falling, twisting and rolling. Jackson felt like he was trying to crawl across the back of a furious, thrashing monster.

Louder. Harder. Louder. Harder.

Crash!

The wooden building on the corner collapsed into a heap.

Boom!

A telephone pole fell to the ground, dragging down wires that sparked and hissed like flaming snakes.

Screams rose above the roar.

And then came a sound so loud, Jackson was sure his ears would explode.

WHHHOOOOSHHHHHHHHHHHHHHH!

People had stopped running and crawling and were staring back toward the loading dock.

The *Chena* seemed to be sinking. And the buildings and docks were crumbling apart and sliding into the harbor. Jackson couldn't understand what he was looking at. Somehow the land was caving in, pouring into the harbor. But how was that possible?

Jackson sat there on the ground, blinking hard. None of this could be real! But every time he opened his eyes, more of the waterfront was gone. The warehouse. The cannery. The cars and trucks. And it wasn't just the waterfront right in front of him. Looking up and down the coast, all the land along the water seemed to be melting away.

Louder. Harder. Louder. Harder.

Jackson slammed his eyes shut. He couldn't watch. He had to get away. And now, through his swirl of panic, all he could think of was Mom and Dad and Uncle Solly.

He started crawling across the street. He'd made it halfway across when . . .

CRACK!

A massive gash opened in the ground right in front of him.

A fissure! Jackson had read about these giant splits in the earth. Never in his life did he think he would see one. He peered down into the blackness. How deep was it? And what was down there? He didn't want to know. He just wanted to get away!

He quickly spun around.

CRACK!

But another gash yawned open.

CRACK!

Jackson sat there, frozen in fear. A sickening stench huffed at him from the earth's open jaws. He squeezed his eyes shut, trying not to imagine what was down there. But his mind flashed with nightmare pictures. Bubbling, burning lava. Shooting flames. The wide-open jaws of a flesh-eating beast.

He felt the ground beneath him start to give way.

No! No! No!

But down Jackson went, screaming, into the darkness.

CHAPTER 13

Oooomph!

Jackson landed on his side on soft, wet sand. The stench made him gag. But his backpack had broken his fall. There was no boiling lava. No flames. He was not inside the mouth of a slobbering beast.

He was at the bottom of a narrow pit.

It was very dark and everything was still shaking. But peering up, Jackson could see the street. He guessed he'd only fallen about six feet.

Might as well be a hundred feet, Jackson thought. Because there was no way to get out. He stretched out his arms, feeling the jagged sides. If a fissure could open up, could it also slam shut? Could he be crushed?

He had to get out of here! But how?

He started to take off his backpack. Maybe he could signal with his flashlight. Or use his rope to somehow pull himself up.

Except before he could get it off, freezing water started to seep up from the ground, soaking his boots. And then . . .

Whoooooooooosh!

Jackson screamed as a blast of freezing water exploded underneath him, a spray so powerful it rocketed him up out of the pit. It was like being shot through the blowhole of a huge whale! The water knocked the air from his lungs. It gushed into his mouth and up his nose.

And then, with a sickening crunch of his ankle, his body landed on the hard, wet street. Pain exploded from the tips of his toes to the top of his leg.

He lay there, too dazed to think.

It took him a long moment to realize that the roaring had stopped. The ground was still.

Finally, the earthquake was over.

Gritting his teeth against the pain in his leg, Jackson managed to sit himself up. He was on the side of the street. Hunks of icy snow mixed with giant rocks had been coughed up from under the ground.

Towers of water blasted up from some of the cracks. The water was brown and smelled rotten, like an outhouse on a hot day. Jackson tried not to think of what was in the water that he'd swallowed.

A man rushed by him carrying a crying little boy in his arms. A woman limped past. He didn't see Leonor or Chris or Nora or Mary. Had they made it off the bridge in time? Were they safe?

Jackson turned and stared in horror at the harbor, blinking in disbelief. Everything that had been there minutes before was gone. All the docks and buildings. All the people who hadn't made it over the bridge in time.

The *Chena* had broken free of its ropes and was drifting in the harbor. Except it wasn't a harbor anymore. It was a swirling sea of wreckage. Everything that had been on the docks was now part of a wild whirlpool. Everything — and everyone.

Panic tore at Jackson's insides. Where were Mom and Dad and Uncle Solly? He had to find them, now! They were at the house they were building. But where was that? Jackson didn't know, and even if he did, he couldn't get there. His ankle was broken, he was sure. The pain was sickening. He could feel it swelling up inside his boot. There was no way he could walk, or even stand.

A hopeless feeling came over Jackson. His mind started to swirl.

Big, hot tears hung in the corners of Jackson's eyes. He tried to brush them away. *Be tough!* he scolded himself.

Get to work!

But his panic only grew.

Get to work.

He said the words over and over to himself. But they just spun around in his mind like the wreckage churning in the harbor. Because what could he do? Mom and Dad had never prepared him for anything like this.

He dragged himself out of the icy puddle where he'd landed. Sucking in his breath and fighting tears, he crawled slowly off the street and into a building that was somehow still standing. He sat there, shivering, his soaked backpack next to him. A strange sound came out of his mouth. Not a scream. Not a sob. It was a weak, rasping cry.

It reminded him of a sound he'd heard before. On the night of the cabin fire. The winter bear had made that sound.

The winter bear.

Now Jackson understood how that bear had felt when it let loose that horrible cry.

Lost.

Terrified.

Totally alone.

CHAPTER 14

And then Jackson heard voices. Familiar voices, calling his name.

"Jackson!"

Leonor?

"Jackson, where are you?"

Chris?

No. Jackson must be hearing things.

But the voices got louder. Closer.

"Jackson!"

Mary? Nora?

Jackson slid out from the doorway. His heart

rose up at the sight of the four kids. They were just down the street, peering into buildings. Looking for something. Looking for . . . Jackson?

"I'm right here!" he shouted.

In a flash they were all around him, crouching down, hovering close. Jackson stared at their faces, which were streaked with dirt and tears. He knew he must look the same.

"We were looking for you!" Leonor said in a ragged voice. Her hair was matted with dirt.

"We saw you fall into that crack!" said Chris. Blood oozed from a deep cut on his cheek.

"We were so scared . . ." Nora said.

"We were praying you got out and you did!" said Mary.

Jackson just stared at them, amazed.

But his relief quickly faded when he saw the look of fear on Leonor's face.

"We have to get out of here," she said breathlessly. "People are saying there's going to be a tsunami."

Tsunamis — massive waves that often happened

after earthquakes. Jackson looked around at the shattered ground, at the collapsed buildings. This was nothing compared to what a powerful tsunami could do. A tsunami could swallow up everything — and everyone — that was left in Valdez.

"Come on," Leonor said, holding out her hand.

But Jackson shook his head.

"I can't walk," he said. "My ankle's broken." He swallowed hard. "You should go."

Each person needed to take care of themselves . . . right?

Chris turned around so that his back was to Jackson. He was ready to run away from here. *Of course he is*, Jackson thought.

But he didn't take off. He lowered himself down right in front of Jackson.

"You can ride on my back," he said.

The next thing Jackson knew, Leonor and Mary had taken hold of his arms. They gently pulled him up. Nora held his back so he wouldn't fall. Keeping his weight off his crushed ankle,

Jackson managed to stand long enough to get himself up onto Chris's back.

"Hold on tight," Leonor said, looping her arm around Jackson's to help hold him up.

As they headed away from the harbor, Jackson turned and saw his backpack lying on the ground.

"Wait —" he started to say. But he stopped himself. There wasn't time to go back.

And besides, what he needed right now wasn't in that backpack.

He tightened his grip on Chris. He looked at Leonor. He felt Mary's and Nora's hands on his back.

And together they ran for their lives.

CHAPTER 15

Jackson gripped his fishing pole, gave it a jiggle. Drops of sweat trickled down his back. It was very hot today — 50 degrees! He shouldn't have worn his flannel shirt. But it was still a perfect summer day in the bush.

Birds chattered from the trees. An eagle soared overhead. Jackson breathed in the familiar summer

83

smells — pine, wildflowers, river water. He looked proudly at the bucket of fish he'd caught for dinner. And then he spotted something moving just across the river. A very large animal.

A grizzly!

Jackson's whole body tensed . . . but then he relaxed.

It was summer, he reminded himself. That bear had plenty of food. The river was wide and deep here, the water rushing fast. Grizzlies were good swimmers. But there was no reason for that bear to make a dangerous journey to cross.

Still, Jackson backed away slowly. He kept his eyes on the bear as he crouched down behind a bush. He sucked in his breath as a flash of pain shot through his ankle. It had mostly healed, thanks to two surgeries in the hospital in Anchorage. But it still ached sometimes.

Jackson watched the bear through the bushes. It was small but looked healthy. Its light-brown fur was thick and glossy. Jackson's mouth dropped open when he noticed that part of the grizzly's ear was missing.

A chill ran up his spine.

Could it be?

The bear turned, and Jackson saw a patch of bare flesh on its back. The skin looked scarred, like it had been burned.

His eyes widened and his heart sped up. *It's you*, Jackson thought.

The winter bear.

Jackson watched in awe as the bear drank from the river. It lifted its big head and looked around. It was enjoying this bright day just like Jackson was. And then it turned and trotted off into the woods.

Jackson barely noticed the tears rolling down his cheeks. That bear had been through so much. But here it was, strong and healthy.

Just like Jackson.

He'd made it through the most powerful earthquake in United States history. The quake had wrecked parts of downtown Anchorage and towns and villages across Alaska. Monster tsunamis smashed into Kodiak, Seward, and Whittier. The worst was in the small village

of Chenega. A wall of water more than 70 feet high practically wiped the village off the earth.

Luckily, the waves that hit Valdez after the quake were just a few feet high. They flooded the downtown, but by then the worst was over. And Jackson and the other kids were safe in Miss Lawrence's car. She'd spotted them as they hurried up Alaska Avenue. She'd driven them out of town, zigzagging around fissures and fallen telephone poles, stopping to pick up other dazed and bloody people.

They wound up at a campsite about six miles from town. Dozens of other people from Valdez had fled to that spot, too. People were terrified that other waves would strike. Or aftershocks — strong jolts that could destroy the buildings already weakened by the first quake.

Jackson's chest got tight as he thought about that long night.

He walked back to the river and splashed his face with the cold river water. But more memories came flooding back. The earsplitting roar of the quake that rang in his ears for days. The desperate voices of people calling out for their children, their parents, their friends. The angry glow of the fires that erupted in Valdez when giant oil tanks exploded. Worst of all was the terror of thinking he might never see Mom or Dad or Uncle Solly again.

One by one, the kids' families had all appeared at the campsite. But by ten o'clock that night, Jackson was still waiting in Miss Lawrence's car. She never left his side, never let go of his hand.

And then finally, there they were, three faces peering through the window of Miss Lawrence's car. Next thing Jackson knew, he was in Mom's arms, with Dad and Uncle Solly huddled close. They explained how Uncle Solly's car had been crushed by a tree. They'd walked for hours looking for Jackson.

"We would have walked forever to find you," Mom had said.

Jackson stepped back from the river and wiped his face with the bottom of his shirt. He took a deep breath and wiped away another round of tears. No use trying to hold them back. Lately, Jackson had realized that even tough people cried sometimes. Even tough people had nightmares and wanted their moms to stay with them until they fell back to sleep. Even tough people froze in panic when a rumble of thunder reminded them of an earthquake. Even tough people needed a friend to carry them when they were too hurt to walk on their own.

Jackson stood there until the swirl of memories faded away. Then he started to pack up his fishing gear. It was getting late. Mom and Dad would be expecting him. Wait until they heard about the winter bear!

They didn't blame the bear for what happened to the cabin. Neither did Jackson. Not anymore. He understood that the creature had just been looking for food. Mom and Dad would be happy to know the bear was healthy and strong. It meant the bear wouldn't go looking for food at people's cabins again.

Not that Jackson or Mom or Dad would ever have to worry about a cabin. Because they weren't rebuilding theirs. They were leaving the bush — for good. They'd decided together that they belonged in Valdez. With Uncle Solly. With their friends. This trip to the bush was just a visit. They'd come for only two weeks. Tomorrow they were heading back to Valdez.

The waterfront was gone. Parts of the town were still badly damaged. And a lot of people had left for good. Like Nora, who was living in Juneau now. She wrote letters to Jackson every week. And Mary, who had moved with her family to Seattle. Jackson missed both of them.

But Leonor's and Chris's families had stayed.

Miss Lawrence, too. Uncle Solly, of course, and plenty of others. They were all working together to rebuild the town. But not in the same place.

In the weeks after the earthquake, scientists came to Valdez. They discovered why all that land along the coast had crumbled away. It turned out it wasn't really *land*. It was a mix of sand and water. When the shaking started, it melted away into the sea. The town's new spot was four miles up the coast, where the ground was solid rock.

"Valdez will rise up again," Uncle Solly had said with his usual pride. "And it will be even better than before."

Jackson picked up his rod and his bucket of fish. He gazed out over the river into the forest. He thought of all the lessons he'd learned growing up here. Most of all, he'd learned how to take care of himself.

But the earthquake had taught Jackson another lesson — that he needed other people, too. He didn't want to be like a grizzly, a fierce creature living alone. He wanted to be like a wolf, part of a pack.

Jackson took one last look around and started back toward the campsite. He loved this wild and beautiful land, and he'd miss living here. But he'd be back to visit, he knew.

And next time, maybe he'd bring his friends.

KEEP READING!

Turn the page to learn more about earthquake science, Alaska history, and the author's research trip to Valdez.

MY JOURNEY TO ALASKA

Hello, dear I Survived readers!

When I was your age, a close friend of mine moved to Anchorage, Alaska. I remember going to my school library and looking for it on a big map of the United States. It took me a few minutes to spot it, a huge state far away from all the others, between Canada and the Pacific Ocean. I remember how my heart sank. I'd never see my friend again, I was sure. There was no way I could ever visit Alaska. My friend might as well be moving to the moon!

It turned out I did see my friend again — she

moved back to Connecticut two years later. But my fascination with the faraway, frozen land of Alaska stayed with me.

And finally, here I am!

As I write this, I'm sitting in the lobby of a hotel in Valdez, Alaska. It's 10:30 at night, but it's still light outside. This time of year — it's early June — the sun doesn't set until nearly midnight. Just a few hours later, the sun will rise again.

My husband, David, came with me and we didn't need a rocket ship to get here — just two airplanes and a car. The plane rides took an entire day, and then it was a six-hour drive from Anchorage to Valdez.

What a journey! David and I kept pulling to the side of the road to stare at the mountains, which looked like they were painted onto the sky. There are mountains all over Alaska — more than in any other state. The highest is Denali, which is more than twenty thousand feet tall.

Rivers are everywhere, too — wide, rushing rivers fed by the melted snow that gushes down from those mountains.

Beautiful mountains and a river on our drive from Anchorage to Valdez.

We dipped our fingers into the freezing water and scooped up gleaming stones that line the riverbeds. Farther down the highway we spotted what looked like a tall frozen river made of jagged blocks of ice. It was a glacier, I knew, one of many in Alaska. This one, the Matanuska Glacier, is twenty-seven miles long. Reading the plaques along the roadside (I love roadside plaques!), I learned more about glaciers — that they once covered much of North America, and that this one was more than 20,000 years old.

The Matanuska Glacier, seen here in the middle of the photo, is 27 miles long and more than 20,000 years old.

More wonders awaited us — fields of wildflowers and crashing waterfalls. We spotted our first moose, nibbling grass at the side of the road. And then, just up ahead, a grizzly!

"*Stop!*" I ordered David. He stopped . . .

. . . Turned out the grizzly was another moose. Oops!

Finally, we reached Valdez. Ringed by the towering Chugach Mountains and perched on the edge of a massive bay called Prince William Sound, Valdez deserves its reputation as the prettiest town in Alaska. It also has some delicious restaurants, a cozy coffee shop, and a health-food market called A Rogue's Garden with blueberry cobbler bars I will be dreaming about for years. And the library is a gem. Thanks to librarian Molly Walker, I got to spend an evening with a big crowd of Valdez kids and their parents.

But of course, I hadn't come to Valdez just to gaze at the breathtaking views, eat cake, and chat with wonderful kids. This was a research trip.

I've traveled to almost every place I've written about in the I Survived series. I've wandered the ancient streets of Pompeii, Italy. I've climbed the slopes of the volcano Mt. St. Helens. I've stood on Civil War battlefields in Gettysburg and climbed down a cliffside in Wellington, Washington, in search of 100-year-old train wreckage. These trips are an important part of my bringing the I Survived books to life. I had come to Alaska to learn more about what happened during and after the 1964 earthquake.

That disaster — a 9.2 earthquake that lasted nearly five minutes — caused destruction and suffering in many areas of Alaska and as far away as California. But early on in my research, I knew I wanted to focus on Valdez. The small city (*very* small — just 650 people lived there at the time of the earthquake) has a fascinating history.

Native Alaskans — Ahtna Athabascan, Sugpiaq, and Eyak — hunted and fished in the areas around Valdez for thousands of years.

More than 700,000 Alaska Native people live in Alaska today. Many still practice their unique traditions. These Athabascan girls are wearing kuspuks — overshirts with large pockets on the front.

In the late 1800s, gold was discovered in Alaska, and tens of thousands of people from the United States and Canada rushed to the state.

Many arrived by ship in Valdez and then set out to find their fortunes.

Few found even a speck of gold. Many froze, starved, drowned, or fell to their deaths on grueling months-long journeys across harsh land, glaciers, and rushing rivers. Exhausted, broke, and frostbit, most left Alaska, vowing never to return.

But some stayed in Valdez, living in tents at first. As time went on, they built houses and schools and churches. They opened shops and restaurants and other businesses. Valdez grew

The first people to live permanently in Valdez arrived during the Gold Rush of 1898.

over the years. By the 1960s, it had become known as a beautiful, vibrant town.

But a deadly danger lurked in Valdez. The ground under the houses and businesses wasn't solid land. It was made up of tiny bits of smashed-up rock, packed tightly together. Nobody knew this . . . until March 27, 1964, when the earthquake struck.

The shaking from the earthquake caused that ground-up rock to turn to mush. That's why the waterfront crumbled into the sea just seconds after the earthquake began. Thirty-two people died in Valdez, more than in any other part of Alaska. Almost all of those who died were standing on the docks.

Small tsunamis flooded the town after the quake. Later that night, big oil tanks exploded, causing fires that burned for days. Amazingly, few houses and buildings in the town were destroyed in the disaster. And at first it seemed the town could quickly recover.

But geologists — scientists who study the earth — recognized that the unstable ground wasn't just near the waterfront. Much of Valdez sat on land that could crumble away if there was another earthquake, even a less powerful one. This is why town leaders made the difficult decision to move the town four miles away, to a spot where the ground was more solid. Within three years, a new Valdez was born.

I learned all about this in the books and articles I read. But I wanted to see it all for myself. I wanted to talk to experts and meet people who survived the quake. And I was in luck. Valdez has an incredible museum — the Valdez Museum and Historical Archive. Two historians there — Faith Revell and Caron Oberg — generously offered to be my guides and to connect me to earthquake survivors still living in the town.

Within ten minutes of arriving in Valdez, I was talking to Tom Gilson, who was thirteen years old when the disaster struck. A fit and friendly retired banker, Tom was born in Valdez and has spent most of his life here. When the earthquake started, Tom was just two blocks from the waterfront. He watched as the *Chena* rose and fell in the churning waters, and as the

Tom Gilson the year before the earthquake

docks crumbled into the sea. "Not a day goes by when I don't think about that day," he told me.

My meeting with Tom took place inside a building owned by the Valdez Museum. The former warehouse is filled with objects from Valdez's history. Most spectacular is an enormous model of "old Valdez" — the town as it stood in its original location, before the earthquake. Spread across six glass-topped tables, the model includes miniature versions of every single house and building. "For people who grew up in old Valdez, this is where we come to talk about our history. Because this is all we've got left of our old town."

Tom Gilson stands at one of the glass-covered tables containing the scale model of the original town of Valdez. He pointed out his family's house and explained that like many buildings in old Valdez, his house was moved to the new town site and still stands. His brother still lives there now. Tom and his wife raised their family in the house next door.

The next day we met Dorothy Moore, who was a nineteen year-old college student when the earthquake struck. A retired teacher and self-taught earthquake expert, Dorothy's eyes sparkled from behind colorful glasses as she welcomed David and me into her home.

Dorothy Moore in high school

We sat in a room filled with books about Alaska history, with paintings of birds and mountains hanging from the walls. Dorothy shared her earthquake experience; she was at home from college when the earthquake struck. The family was sitting down to a spaghetti dinner when the house started to shake violently.

Like most Alaskans, she'd experienced earthquakes before. "But never anything like this," she said. The shaking got stronger . . . and didn't stop. "Most earthquakes last for less than a minute. This one lasted five. I never thought it would end."

As we sat together, Dorothy didn't dwell on the day of the disaster. A lifelong teacher, she was eager to share her knowledge of earthquake science and disaster preparedness. She gave me files filled with scientific articles, maps, and lesson plans.

She explained more about the town's new location. It's definitely safer than old Valdez, she told me. But earthquakes and tsunamis are still a big risk here (and everywhere in Alaska). So it's important to be prepared. She keeps her house stocked with candles and other emergency supplies. She knows how to reach high ground in case an earthquake triggers a tsunami.

Dorothy's home is like a museum, packed with books, articles, and other materials about Alaska history and the earthquake. She explained that Valdez is still prone to earthquakes and tsunamis, but its new location is far safer than the first.

"You don't have to be scared," Dorothy said. "But you can know how to stay safe."

David and I spent four wonderful days in Valdez. A highlight was when Faith and Caron, the historians from the Valdez Museum, drove us to the site of old Valdez. There's almost nothing left — some rotten wood stumps that were once part of a pier, a rusted forklift, a concrete slab where the post office once stood.

A few days later, David and I returned on our own. I walked to the edge of the water. It looked

During our trip to the waterfront of old Valdez, Faith (right) shared fascinating details about the town's history and the events of the earthquake.

beautiful and peaceful. Birdsong echoed through the air. But I felt a deep ache in my chest as I thought about what happened here. The terror of those five minutes. The people who were lost. The sorrow of those left behind.

But as I turned away from the water, I thought of Tom Gilson and Dorothy Moore. Both have spent most of their lives in Valdez. They're proud of the town's history, and they love living there.

Like so many places I have visited to research I Survived books, the waterfront in old Valdez is a beautiful place, haunted by tragedy.

Tom and Dorothy reminded me of other people I've met on other I Survived trips. Tornado survivors from Joplin, Missouri. Hurricane survivors from New Orleans, Louisiana. Fire survivors from Paradise, California. Holocaust survivors from World War II.

I've learned so much from these people, who have generously shared their stories and insights with me. Their most important lessons are not about history or natural disasters but about how we can move forward after experiencing even unimaginable losses. We don't forget the past. Our losses leave scars. But with the help of our families and friends, we can rebuild our towns — and our lives — on solid ground.

MORE FACTS ABOUT EARTHQUAKES

THE 1964 ALASKA EARTHQUAKE WAS THE MOST POWERFUL EVER RECORDED IN UNITED STATES HISTORY

The quake had a magnitude of 9.2. That makes it the strongest ever measured in North America and the second most powerful in the world. The strongest happened just a few years before, off the coast of Chile.

Not only was the Alaska earthquake shockingly strong, it lasted a very long time — almost five minutes. History's most famous US earthquake, the San Francisco earthquake of 1906, lasted 60 seconds.

As I was researching this book, I kept trying to imagine more than four minutes of shaking, roaring ... screaming. To those who survived, those five minutes must have felt like forever.

The earthquake struck off the coast of Alaska, under Prince William Sound, a 2,500-square-mile area of ocean along Alaska's south-central coast. Shock waves exploded in every direction. The most violent shaking was felt in Anchorage, Valdez, Seward, and other areas along the south-central coast of the state. Twelve hundred miles away, the famous building called the Space Needle swayed in Seattle. Fishermen in Louisiana even noticed strange ripples in lakes and rivers.

In some areas of Alaska, the ground shattered apart. In this Anchorage neighborhood, houses also slid into the sea.

*Alaska's biggest city, Anchorage, was severely damaged in the earthquake.
On this downtown street, parts of the ground dropped eleven feet.*

Fissures like this one split the ground throughout Alaska's southern coast.

THE ALASKA EARTHQUAKE WAS
FOLLOWED BY TSUNAMIS

In the minutes following the Alaska earthquake, tsunami (tsoo-NAH-mee) waves smashed into cities and towns along parts of Alaska's coastline. These waves caused tremendous destruction and more deaths than the actual earthquake.

The first tsunamis to hit were caused by underwater landslides and "slumps" — areas where the land at the edge of a waterfront slid into the sea from the shaking. This is what happened in Valdez.

The tsunami in Valdez was just a few feet high. But others were massive. One wave, more than seventy feet tall, swallowed the small village of Chenega, killing twenty-six out of the seventy-five people living there.

Other tsunamis began farther out in the ocean in the Gulf of Alaska. Over the six hours following the quake, waves sped out in many directions. Some hit along the coast of Alaska. Others raced down the west coast of the United States at more than four hundred miles per hour — faster than some jets. Four people died when waves crashed ashore in Oregon. An hour later, twelve people drowned in waves that hit Crescent City, California. Waves reached as far as Hawaii and Japan, thousands of miles away from where they began.

Tsunami damage in the town of Kodiak, Alaska

131 PEOPLE DIED IN THE ALASKA EARTHQUAKE AND TSUNAMI

This loss of life was tragic. But far *fewer* people died in the Alaska earthquake than in other recent powerful earthquakes and tsunamis. This is because Alaska was (and still is) mostly wilderness.

The state of Alaska is more than twice the size of Texas. But in 1964, only about 250,000 people lived in the entire state. Today, approximately 733,000 people live in Alaska. But still, less than 1 percent of the land is occupied by humans. Millions of acres are set aside for wildlife.

Had a similar earthquake and tsunami struck a more crowded and built-up area, the death toll would have been far higher. For example, the great Tohoku earthquake and tsunami of 2011 devastated parts of Japan. That disaster killed about 18,000 people.

Damage in Otsochi, Japan, following the 2011 earthquake and tsunami

EARTHQUAKES WERE ONCE
A MYSTERY

Nearly two thousand years ago, when the volcano Vesuvius erupted near Naples, Italy, most people believed the explosive terror was the work of furious gods or goddesses or a massive beast waking up inside the mountain.

That's not because those people were foolish. Back then, scientists had not yet begun to understand the forces that create volcanic eruptions, earthquakes, and other natural disasters.

Slowly, over the centuries, Earth scientists — known as geologists — began to more fully understand our fascinating planet so that people no longer blamed goddesses or monsters for disasters.

In the 1910s and 1920s, scientists began to make important breakthroughs in earthquake science. This is when geologists first came up with a theory known as **plate tectonics**. To understand it, first picture our big, beautiful planet Earth floating in space. But Earth is not just a gigantic ball of solid rock covered with oceans and land. Our planet is made up of four main layers — the crust, the mantle, and the outer and inner cores.

The crust, the outer part, is made of rock, and it's what you are sitting on top of right now. The crust is between about four and about forty miles thick, and is covered with oceans, mountains, and our cities and towns. It is broken up into seventeen giant slabs (called **plates**) that fit together like pieces of a puzzle.

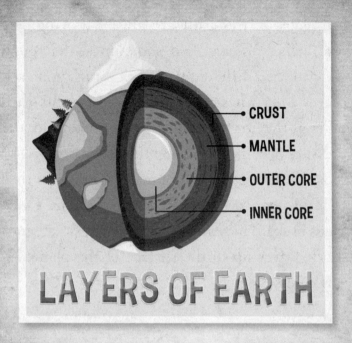

CRUST
MANTLE
OUTER CORE
INNER CORE

LAYERS OF EARTH

You can think of Earth's crust like a cracked, crunchy chocolate coating wrapped around a ball of gooey caramel. The places where the plates meet (imagine the cracks in the chocolate) are called **plate boundaries**. The crust sits on top of Earth's mantle, an even thicker layer of molten rock (the caramel!).

What does this have to do with earthquakes?

According to the **theory of plate tectonics**,

the plates of the crust are always moving — a few inches a year. And sometimes, the rough edges of two different plates get "stuck" on each other. The plates push and grind against each other as they try to keep moving. Sometimes the pressure becomes so strong that one of the plates slips violently past, over, or under the other. Or they suddenly snap back to their original positions. These kinds of sharp movements release energy that sends shock waves up to the surface of the planet — earthquakes.

The map above is a world map that also shows all the different plates. These plates are outlined in black, and they each have names. Very large earthquakes almost always happen at plate boundaries — the places where the plates meet. The circle on this map shows where the 1964 Alaska earthquake happened. Earthquakes can also happen in cracks in the plates. The places where earthquakes happen — both plate boundaries and other cracks in the plates — are known as "faults."

SCIENTISTS LEARNED FROM THE ALASKA EARTHQUAKE

Not all geologists agreed with the theory of plate tectonics at first. But that would change in the months after the Alaska earthquake.

The US government sent a geologist named George Plafker to Alaska. He and other scientists spent months walking across the shattered land.

They measured fissures. They discovered places where the quake had caused flat land to rise by nearly 40 feet. In other places, the land dropped down. Entire forests had been killed by seawater.

Most intriguing to Plafker, rocks along the shoreline were covered with barnacles. Those are tiny sea creatures that cling to rocks and other surfaces underwater. But these barnacles were all dead.

Plafker realized this was a sign that the earthquake had caused the seafloor to rise up so that the barnacles were no longer covered with water. This caused the tiny creatures to dry up.

In this photo from 2013, George Plafker shows a picture of the Alaskan shoreline after the quake. The white stripe on the rocks is dried-up barnacles, proving that the sea floor rose up during the earthquake.

Like detectives solving a mystery, the scientists put together their clues. Their work helped prove the theory of plate tectonics. They made new discoveries about where the biggest earthquakes are likely to happen — and ideas for making us safer. We can't prevent Earth from shaking under our feet, but we can try to be prepared.

Today, buildings in earthquake-prone areas like Alaska and California have laws to make sure buildings and bridges are constructed to withstand earthquakes. Kids at school go through earthquake drills so they know how to stay safe.

Third graders take cover under their desks during an earthquake drill in California.

The Alaska earthquake of 1964 may not be the most famous earthquake. (It was an I Survived reader named Nathan who suggested the topic to me! Thank you, Nathan!) But to geologists, what was learned from the Alaska earthquake makes it one of the most important in history.

SOMEWHERE IN THE WORLD, AN EARTHQUAKE IS PROBABLY HAPPENING RIGHT NOW

Hundreds of earthquakes happen every single day. Most are so mild that even people living right near them don't feel anything. But every year, between six and twenty of those earthquakes are strong enough to cause serious damage. And every few years there is an earthquake somewhere that causes enormous destruction.

Some places are more prone to earthquakes than others. Many of history's most destructive quakes have happened in areas that border the Pacific Ocean. This horseshoe-shaped region is known as the Ring of Fire. There are more active volcanoes (over 450!) here than anywhere in the world. And several big tectonic plates come together in the area, which is why so many earthquakes — 90 percent of all earthquakes on Earth — happen somewhere along the Ring of Fire.

In the United States, Alaska gets more earthquakes than any other state. California comes in second. Washington and Oregon are also in the top ten. No surprise, all these states are on the Ring of Fire.

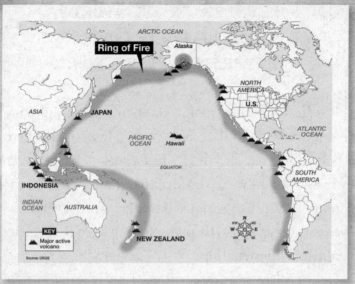

Ninety percent of all earthquakes happen along the Ring of Fire, shown here by the gray shading. The circle represents the 1964 Alaska earthquake.

HOW TO STAY SAFE IN AN EARTHQUAKE

Parts of the world are more prone to earthquakes than others. In the United States, the top spots are along the West Coast — Alaska, California, Washington, and Oregon.

But we should all know what to do if an earthquake strikes. I live in Connecticut but many years ago found myself in a strong earthquake in Los Angeles, California.

I wasn't yet writing I Survived. But I did know something about earthquakes — enough to know how to stay safe.

And you can, too. Here's how to get started —
and learn more.

1. KNOW THE SAFEST SPOTS

If an earthquake strikes, you will have a few
seconds to find safety. If you are inside, try to go to
a room that is deep inside your house, away from
windows. Bathrooms and closets often work well.

If you are outside, try to get to an open area
away from buildings, telephone poles, and other
big structures. Being near a building is especially
dangerous since people can be hit by falling
debris and glass.

2. DROP, COVER, HOLD ON

If you are in an earthquake at school or at home,
drop down to the ground and try to take cover
under something strong. A table or a desk can
work. With one arm, hold tight to the leg of the
table or desk. Put your other arm over your head
and neck. Stay there until the shaking has stopped.

| DROP! | COVER! | HOLD ON! |

Most schools have earthquake drills, so you have probably practiced this. But do it at home, too.

3. IF YOU LIVE NEAR THE OCEAN, FIND HIGHER GROUND

Tsunamis can happen within minutes of an earthquake. If you are near the ocean, get to high ground as quickly as possible. Many communities have a tsunami plan — make sure you know it. Often there are signs showing where to go. If not, try to get to the top of a very high hill (at least 100 feet higher than the sea). If you can't do that,

walk as quickly as you can away from the water.
Try to get at least a mile from the coast.

4. MAKE A FAMILY PLAN

If you live in a place prone to quakes, talk to
your family about a plan. If you're at home
when it happens, where would you all go? Do
you have an earthquake "go bag"? This is a
bag of important things that are already packed
so you and your family can make a quick
escape — medicine, some money, a change of
clothes, and other necessities.

If you're not together, decide where you will all

meet, or who you will call — a family member or friend who lives outside of your area is ideal.

5. MEMORIZE IMPORTANT PHONE NUMBERS

If you are old enough to have your own phone, chances are important numbers are in there. So, you don't need to know them by heart, right? Wrong! You could lose your phone, or it could go dead when you need it most. Also, cell service often goes out when a natural disaster strikes. That's why you need to also store important phone numbers . . . in your brain! These include numbers for members of your family, a trusted neighbor, and that all-important family friend I mentioned above.

6. HELP THOSE IN NEED

When a big earthquake strikes, people can lose their homes and all their belongings. You, your family, and your friends can help them by donating money and other supplies. Make sure you are working with a good organization who will guarantee that donations make it into the hands of people who need them most.

Some suggestions:
Save the Children
savethechild.org
American Red Cross
redcross.org
World Vision
worldvision.org

A Red Cross worker distributes supplies following a 2010 earthquake in Haiti.

LEARN MORE

The United States Geological Survey created a resource that is packed with facts, history, and earthquake tips for kids:

Earthquake.USGS.gov

You can also check my website for ideas on how to help people who have been impacted by natural disasters and other challenging events:

LaurenTarshis.com

SELECTED BIBLIOGRAPHY

HERE ARE SOME OF THE BOOKS THAT HELPED ME RESEARCH THIS BOOK

Bad Friday: The Great & Terrible 1964 Earthquake, by Lew Freedman, Epicenter Press, 2018

Coming into the Country, by John McPhee, Farrar, Straus and Giroux, 1977

"The 1964 Great Alaska Earthquake and Tsunamis — A Modern Perspective and Enduring Legacies," by Thomas M. Brocher, John R. Filson, Gary S. Fuis, Peter J. Haeussler, Thomas L. Holzer, George Plafker,

and J. Luke Blair, United States Geological Survey:
Perspectives on a Changing World, March 2014

*The Great Quake: How the Biggest Earthquake in North
America Changed Our Understanding of the Planet*, by
Henry Fountain, Crown, 2017

Indigenous Continent: The Epic Contest for North America,
by Pekka Hamalainan, W. W. Norton, 2022

*This Is Chance: The Shaking of an All-American City, a
Voice That Held It Together*, by Jon Mooallem, Random
House, 2020

Valdez Rising, by Tabitha Gregory, Sapphire Mountain
Books, 2022

FURTHER READING

OTHER I SURVIVED BOOKS ABOUT EARTHQUAKES AND VOLCANOES

I Survived the San Francisco Earthquake, 1906
I Survived the Japanese Tsunami, 2011
I Survived the Destruction of Pompeii, AD 79
I Survived the Eruption of Mount St. Helens, 1980

Lauren poses on Alaska's Glenn Highway, near the Matanuska Glacier.

Lauren Tarshis's *New York Times* bestselling I Survived series tells stories of young people and their resilience and strength in the midst of unimaginable disasters and times of turmoil. Lauren has brought her signature warmth, integrity, and exhaustive research to topics such as the September 11 attacks, the American Revolution, Hurricane Katrina, the bombing of Pearl Harbor, and other world events. Lauren lives in Connecticut with her family, and can be found online at laurentarshis.com.